The Wizard

WRITTEN BY

Bill Martin Jr

ILLUSTRATED BY

Alex Schaefer

Harcourt Brace & Company

SAN DIEGO   NEW YORK   LONDON

For my friend the wizard, Lee Savell
  —B.M.

To my family for their love and support
  —A.S.

Requests for permission to make copies
of any part of the work should be mailed to:
Permissions Department, Harcourt Brace & Company,
6277 Sea Harbor Drive,
Orlando, Florida 32887-6777.

Library of Congress Cataloging-in-Publication Data
Martin, Bill, 1916–
The Wizard/Bill Martin Jr; illustrated by Alex Schaefer.—1st ed.
p. cm.
Summary: A wizard and his assistants cast a spell that
ends up making the wizard disappear.
ISBN 0–15–298926–9
[1. Wizards—Fiction.   2. Magic—Fiction.   3. Stories in rhyme.]
I. Schaefer, Alex, 1969–   ill. II. Title
PZ8.3.M4113Wi   1994
[E]—dc20   93-15521

PRINTED IN SINGAPORE

The illustrations in this book were done in oil on linen.
The display type was set in Remedy Double and the text type
was set in Bembo and Remedy Double by the Photocomposition
Center, Harcourt Brace & Company, San Diego, California.
Color separations were made by Bright Arts, Ltd., Singapore.
Printed and bound by Tien Wah Press, Singapore
This book was printed with soya-based inks on Leykam recycled
paper, which contains more than 20 percent postconsumer waste and
has a total recycled content of at least 50 percent.
Production supervision by Warren Wallerstein and David Hough
Designed by Trina Stahl

I dance. I sing.

I twinkle.

I wing.

I flip.

I flop.

I dee-dip.

I pong.

I ding.

I slide.

I slip.

Oops!

I stumble!

I tumble!

I crumble!

Talley-oop!

I zipper-zoop!

I disappear!